Type 1 DiaBitsies

MEET THE TYPE 1 DIABITSIES

GEAR

ADVENTURE GEAR

SNACKS

Amy Hernandez Greenbank

Find activities, recipes, updates, and more at Type1DiaBitsies.com

Send questions or comments to info@typeldiabitsies.com

ISBN 978-0-578-47827-2

The information provided in this book is not meant to be used, nor should it be used, to diagnose or treat any medical condition. For diagnosis or treatment of any medical problem, consult your physician.

For Bella and Lily,
who cheered for every page and brought
me juice when I was low.

Welcome to the world of the Type 1 DiaBitsies! Today, the Bitsies are going on a food adventure. Let's meet the explorers!

Insulin Joe

Likes: **Helping his friends**

Dislikes: **Really hot days**

Fun Facts:

Joe loves to laugh. Tap out his bubbles to make him giggle.

Joe likes to stay cool and lives in the fridge until his pals are ready for his help.

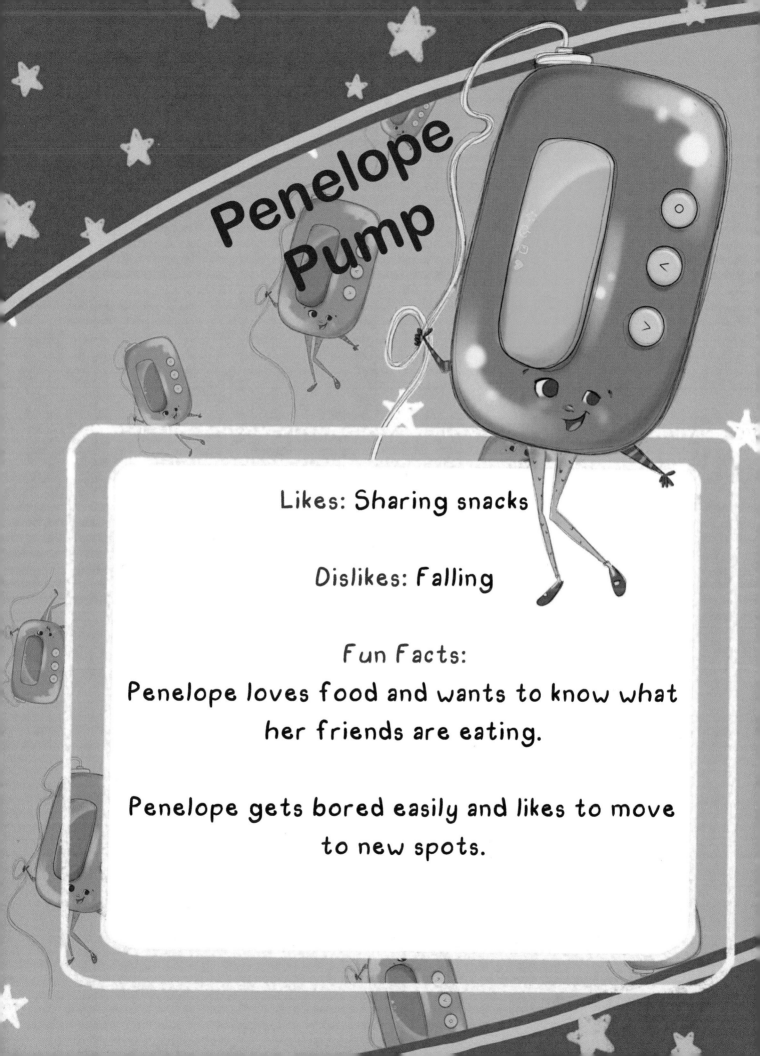

Penelope Pump

Likes: Sharing snacks

Dislikes: Falling

Fun Facts:
Penelope loves food and wants to know what her friends are eating.

Penelope gets bored easily and likes to move to new spots.

Meter Pete

Likes: Countdowns!
5...4...3...2...1...Blastoff!

Dislikes: Low batteries

Fun Facts:
Pete is a real joker and loves to tickle your finger tips.

Pete has many test strip pals. They are sneaky and like to hide in small spaces.

Jenny Pen

Likes: Wearing caps

Dislikes: Feeling empty

Fun Facts:
Like Penelope, Jenny likes to move to different spots.

Jenny loves her caps, and wears a new one each time she sees her friends.

"Alright! Everyone have their maps? Helmets? Snacks? Let's go!" exclaims Joe.

"First, we are going to the Juicy Jungle. Look, an apple ape! A pineapple parrot!"

"Hey!" shouts Pete, "That tomato toucan took my map!"

"No worries," says Joe, "I still have mine. Let's go this way. Is that mud?"

"Super sticky mud," replies Penelope, "and I'm sinking in it!"
"This must be the Snack Time Swamp," says Joe.

"Woah, it's an animal cracker alligator!" cries Pete.

"Wait a minute. An alligator. With sharp teeth. Run!"

"Let's go this way," says Joe, pointing at his map.
"It looks like water."

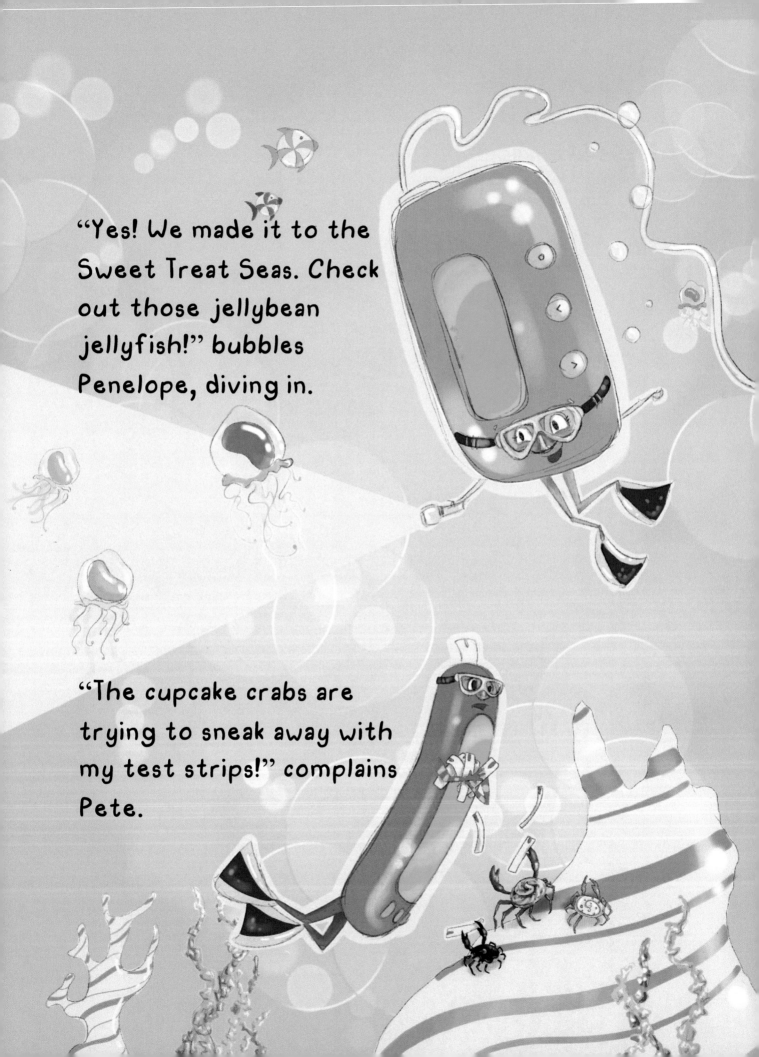

"Yes! We made it to the Sweet Treat Seas. Check out those jellybean jellyfish!" bubbles Penelope, diving in.

"The cupcake crabs are trying to sneak away with my test strips!" complains Pete.

"Yuck! I'm covered in sugar sprinkle sand!" shouts Jenny.

"Maybe we aren't supposed to have adventures. Maybe things like fruit, cupcakes, and animal crackers are for people without diabetes," sniffs Jenny.

"No way!" exclaims Joe. "We can still have our favorite things and keep having awesome adventures. We just need to plan ahead."

"Pete, here are some extra test strips."

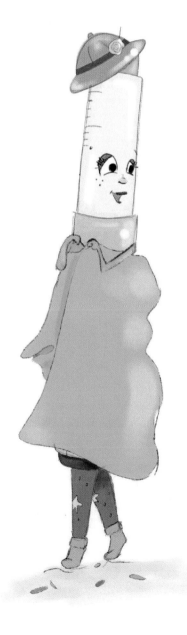

"Jenny, I brought some towels, just in case."

"So we can still have the things we love?" asks Penelope.

"Even cupcakes?" asks Jenny.

"Of course!" laughs Joe. "And we can keep on exploring!"

"I can't wait for our next adventure!" exclaims Pete.

EXPLORER'S JOURNAL

By the Type 1

DiaBitsies

ALL ABOUT ME

BY INSULIN JOE

My job is to help people with diabetes.

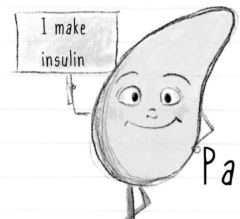

I make insulin

Everybody has a pancreas inside their belly.

Pancreas

The pancreas makes insulin to let energy into your body.

Sorry, no insulin today

Sometimes, it stops working the way it should, and that can make people sick.

So I come to the

RESCUE!

ME!

People with
diabetes
take insulin when
they eat, and get what
they need from their
food!

SUPER!

Cool!

ALL ABOUT ME!

By Penelope Pump

 I give my pals insulin.

I have a small tube that pumps insulin into a diabetic person's skin without pain!

tube **Beach Day!**

Most times,
when someone eats,
they need insulin.

— Insulin Joe

When I know what my pal is going to eat, I give just the right amount.

YUM!

All about Me
By
Jenny Pen

I am an insulin pen. My friends say I look like a regular pen, but my job is really different.

I hold insulin until my diabetic friends need it.

When it's time to eat,
a person with diabetes decides
how much insulin they need
        and then turns my dial to
choose the right amount.

With a tiny prick
to the skin, I
give my pals the
insulin they need!

ALL ABOUT ME

By Meter Pete

I am curious and like to check up on my diabetic pals.

DOING OK?

People with diabetes need to check their blood sugar levels. So I help.

Check it out

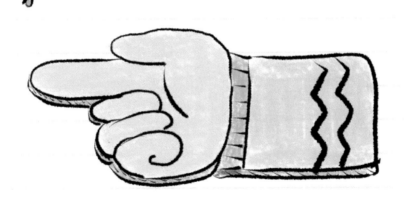

I give a small prick to a pal's finger and then take a tiny amount of blood.

From this little drop, I can tell how high or low a friend's blood sugar levels are.

I think I'm pretty smart!

Thank you for exploring with us! See you soon!

Joe

Penelope

Jenny

Pete

Parent Guide

Type 1 Diabetes comes with lots of new words and tools. It can be overwhelming for a child. Help to take some of the fear away and find the fun.

Be creative when using your child's supplies.
Try these fun suggestions:

- Let your child help you prepare supplies.
- When filling insulin, let your child gently tap to tickle Joe and eliminate bubbles.
- When entering carb counts into your child's pump, talk to Penelope aloud. Tell her what your child is eating and ask if she likes that food.
- At an infusion sight change, tell Penelope that she can now get up and move around. What is her favorite spot?
- When bringing out your child's insulin pen, chat with Jenny. Ask her where she'd like to go.
- While taking blood sugar readings, have your child count backward while you administer the finger stick. Take turns telling Pete silly jokes.

Most of all, try to relax and keep things positive!

Made in the USA
Monee, IL
06 February 2021